Fishing

Annette Smith

Illustrated by Richard Hoit

On Monday

I went fishing
with my mom.

On Tuesday

I went fishing
with my dad.

On Wednesday

I went fishing
with my big sister.

7

On Thursday

I went fishing

with my big brother.

On Friday

I went fishing
with my family.

On Saturday

I went fishing

with my grandma.

Look at my **fish!**

On Sunday

I went fishing

with my grandma again.